W9-CAB-624

little bee books

An imprint of Bonnier Publishing USA
251 Park Avenue South, New York, NY 10010
Copyright © 2018 by Little Bee Books
All rights reserved, including the right of reproduction in whole or in part in any form.
Little Bee Books is a trademark of Bonnier Publishing USA, and associated colophon is a trademark of Bonnier Publishing USA.
Library of Congress Cataloging-in-Publication Data is available upon request.
Printed in the United States of America LAK 0318
ISBN 978-1-4998-0587-1 (hc)
First Edition 10 9 8 7 6 5 4 3 2 1
ISBN 978-1-4998-0586-4 (pb)
First Edition 10 9 8 7 6 5 4 3 2 1
littlebeebooks.com
bonnierpublishingusa.com

THE MAJOR EIGHTS

THE GOO DISASTER!

by Melody Reed
illustrated by Émilie Pépin

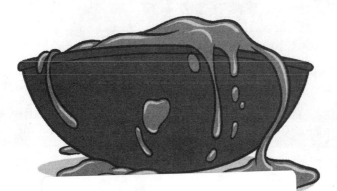

CONTENTS

1. SOUND OF STARDUST 1

2. THE D+ 7

3. KEVIN 13

4. A BIG MESS 19

5. A BIGGER MESS 29

6. GLITTER, MUD, AND FLYING GOO ... 37

7. DRUM SOLO 47

8. THE GOO GOES AWOL 53

9. DANCING GOO 65

10. BEHIND THE CURTAIN 71

11. THE BEST SURPRISE 83

SOUND OF STARDUST

Becca waved a few pieces of paper above her head. "I got it!" she shouted.

Mr. Barrett, the librarian, hushed her.

Even though Becca, Jasmine, Scarlet, and I are all in different classes, the entire third grade has library time together.

"Got what?" I whispered. I set my books down.

Scarlet grinned. "The new Silver Sporks song!"

"That's great!" Jasmine whispered. "Is it for us to play?"

Becca nodded. She passed out copies to the three of us. "Scarlet and I thought we could play something new for the Arts Banquet. I've looked at the guitar chords. It should be easy to play."

At the talent show last Friday, our band, the Major Eights, had won the chance to perform at the big event, along with two other acts from the competition. Grown-ups paid a lot of money to go to the banquet, and the money would help the arts program at our school.

I couldn't wait. My dad was in the navy. He'd been gone for six months and had never seen our band perform. Mom was going to film a video of it to send to him.

"I already know the words," Scarlet chimed in.

"Let me see the piano part," said Jasmine. She studied the music. "I'll have to practice, but I can learn it in time for the banquet. How about you, Maggie?"

I pulled the paper close, examining it. " 'Sound of Stardust' . . . I love this song!" I squealed. "It has an amazing drum solo." I flipped to the next page and my face fell. As cool as it sounded, the drum solo looked hard.

My friends didn't notice.
"Great!" said Becca.
"Fantastic!" said Scarlet.
"Awesome!" said Jasmine.
"Shhhhhh!!!" said Mr. Barrett.

2

THE D+

My feet would not keep still. I squeezed my pencil. I bounced in my seat.

Mr. Caldera was handing out our graded science tests. But I couldn't stop thinking about the Arts Banquet.

Finally, Mr. Caldera slid a piece of paper in front of me.

I blinked. "Um," I began. "Mr. Caldera?"

"Yes, Maggie?"

I pointed to the big, red D+ on the upper right-hand corner. "All my answers were right."

But Mr. Caldera didn't say it was the wrong grade. He just turned the paper over to the other side.

It was filled with questions! Questions I hadn't answered. I slapped my forehead.

Mr. Caldera cleared his throat. "I take it that you forgot there was another side to the test."

I nodded again. I'd been thinking about the talent show when I took the test. I hadn't been paying attention to the directions.

Mr. Caldera frowned. "I can't give you another chance on the test. I told everyone in the class to turn the paper over for the rest of the questions. But you can still enter the science fair. If you do well there, it will boost your grade."

My shoulders slumped.

"Kevin is your neighbor, right? He's doing the science fair, too. You can work together if you want."

I looked at Kevin. He'd always lived next door, but we'd never really been friends.

"Here," Mr. Caldera said. He gave me a printout from a website. "This website has good ideas for science projects. Let me know if you need any help."

"Thanks," I mumbled.

"Oh, and congrats on the talent show," he added. "I can't wait to see the Major Eights again at the banquet!"

Mr. Caldera moved on. I studied the printout.

The science fair was two days after the Arts Banquet! I had a tricky drum solo to learn. Now I had a science project, too. How was I going to have time to do both?

3

KEViN

The school bus creaked to a stop.

"Practice tonight?" Jasmine asked as we all got off the bus. "We could try the new song."

Kevin was waiting for me on the sidewalk.

"I can't," I said.

Jasmine shrugged. "It's okay. Scarlet's at the café, anyway. Maybe tomorrow."

My shoulders sagged. "Maybe."

I caught up with Kevin.

"So, science project," he said. "Do you want to work together? Like Mr. Caldera said?"

Jasmine and Becca walked home together. They were going to practice the song. I was sure of it.

"What am I going to do?" I wailed.

"What's wrong?" Kevin asked. "We have two whole weeks."

"Yeah," I said. "But the Arts Banquet is also in two weeks. How can I practice and do a science project?"

He nodded. "Oh yeah. That's right. Good job at the talent show."

"Thanks," I mumbled.

"I play the drums too," he said.

"Really?"

"Really." Kevin paused. "Hey, I know! We should do a project with drums!"

I glared at him. "It's a science project. Not a *music* project."

He shuffled his feet. "Well, music is science, right?"

"No, it isn't. It's music."

"Well, we have to pick a project. What do you want to do?"

I pulled out the paper with the website. "I'll ask my mom to help me look one up tonight."

"Okay. But it's got to be messy."

"What?"

"Good science projects are usually pretty messy." He smiled.

"Uh, okay . . ."

"See you tomorrow after school!" Kevin waved and went home.

I wrinkled my nose. This kid thought music and science were the same thing. And he liked messes. Maybe we weren't such a good fit after all. But at least it would be less work to have a partner. Less time on science, more time on "Sound of Stardust."

A BIG MESS

During computer lab the next day, I typed in the web address Mr. Caldera had recommended. A page with pictures of beakers popped up. Below the header was a list of science projects. Soft eggshells, bean plants, a solar oven . . . These projects would all take too much time. Time I needed to spend working on my drum solo.

"There must be something quick."

I clicked the next link: Non-Newtonian Fluid. Whatever that was.

I read it. "Goo: Both a liquid and a solid."

That wasn't possible.

I kept reading. Just two ingredients! And there was a picture of white goop on a kid's hand. Yuck! Well, Kevin would be happy.

But best of all, next to preparation time, the website said just five minutes!

I bounced in my seat.

I'd found us a science fair project!

After school, I met up with Kevin in the science lab.

"Let me know if you need any help," Mr. Caldera said from his desk, where he was grading quizzes.

"Thank you," I said.

Mr. Caldera had already pulled out cornstarch and a bowl for us to use for our project.

Kevin filled a beaker full of water. "So . . ." he said, "we just mix these together?"

"Yep." I dumped some cornstarch into the bowl.

Kevin added the water to the bowl, as white powder puffed up around us. "Well, it's messy enough," he said with a smile.

I checked my watch. If this really took five minutes, I'd still have time to get home and practice the solo today.

But the goo looked too chalky. When I stirred the sludge, the spoon kept getting stuck to it.

"Argh!" I shouted. "I can't—"

Kevin rolled up his sleeves.

"What are you doing?" I asked.

"Kneading it, like bread." Kevin plunged his hands in. "It's only cornstarch and water."

I frowned. "But it looks gross."

"Whoa! Check this out," said Kevin. Sure enough, the goo slid off his fingers. Just like in the picture from the website.

"It looks like glue," I said.

"But it doesn't feel like glue. You've got to try this!"

I sighed. I set down the spoon and stuck my hands in.

At first, it was still too powdery. I scraped some of the starch out with my fingers so I could mix it in better. But when I opened my hand, the goo slipped back into the bowl in strings!

"It's hard when you squeeze it," said Kevin. "And it drips out when you open your hand."

"Both a liquid and a solid," I said. "All done!" I announced.

Mr. Caldera came over to our table and raised an eyebrow. "What is it?"

"It's, um . . . goo." I poked it to show him.

"Mmm," said Mr. Caldera. "But what's your variable?"

"What do you mean?"

"Well, a science experiment has to have a variable. That's the thing you change so you can see what its effect on your project is."

Kevin and I frowned.

"I'm sure you'll think of something," Mr. Caldera said.

5

A BIGGER MESS

When I got home from school, I found everyone in our kitchen. Mom was making dinner, my nana was singing to some music with my youngest sister Morgan, who's two, and Megan, who's five, was coloring at the table.

"Maggie!" she shouted when I came in. She ran over and tugged at my hands. "Come color with me!"

"I can't tonight, Megan," I said, feeling nervous about the science fair project. I had to think of a variable.

Megan pouted, curling up her lower lip. "Come play, Maggie!" she whined.

Nana shut off the music, and Morgan began to whimper. But before Morgan could really begin wailing, Nana whisked her out of her high chair and reached for Megan's hand.

"Come on, you two, dinner is almost ready. Let's go wash up." She left with both my sisters.

I sighed in relief. Sometimes our house can feel like a zoo! Mom says we're lucky we have Nana. I love Nana. But I miss my dad, too.

"How did your experiment go, honey?" Mom asked when it was quiet.

I shrugged.

"I got an email from Mr. Caldera today. This project is important for your science grade, right?"

I nodded. "Yeah."

"And the science fair is only two days after the banquet. Is that right?"

I didn't like where this was going. "Um . . . right."

"I know you're looking forward to the banquet, sweetie. But I can't let you perform unless your project is done by then."

My mouth dropped open.

"I'm sorry, honey. School is more important. The Major Eights may have to play without you."

"Mom!"

She shook her head. "No arguments, Maggie."

I flopped my head on the table. If I didn't play at the Arts Banquet, I couldn't send a video of it to Dad!

We had to figure out this project. And fast!

6

GLiTTER, MUD, AND FLYING GOO

Kevin and I stood on the sidewalk two days later, which was Saturday. Only a week left until the Arts Banquet. Becca, Jasmine, and Scarlet had come to help us with the project. At our feet were five bowls of goo, one for each of us.

"Okay, is everybody ready?" I asked.

Jasmine held silver glitter above her bowl, Scarlet held a bunch of grass, and Becca held some dry cereal. I held pieces of ripped-up paper. Kevin held a handful of dirt.

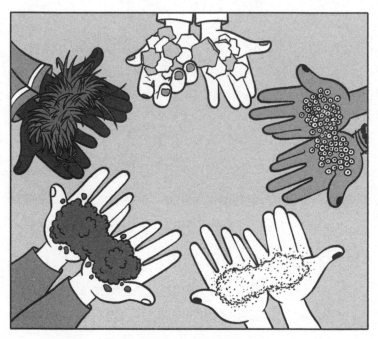

"Ready," they all said.
"Go!" I shouted.

We each opened our hands over our bowls of goo. The bits of paper I dropped looked like snowflakes. As soon as the pieces of paper landed on the goo, I thrust my hands down to mix it together.

"Ooh, mine's pretty," said Jasmine, her hands sparkly from the glitter.

"Gross!" said Scarlet and Becca, looking at their bowls.

"Awesome!" shouted Kevin, muddy goo dripping from his fingers.

"Hey, guess what?" said Jasmine. Glitter goo dripped from both of her hands. "I think I've learned the piano part of the Silver Sporks song." She grinned.

"That's great!" said Becca. "How about you, Maggie? How's the drum solo coming?"

"It's . . . going okay." I bit my lip. To be honest, the solo sounded like my littlest sister banging on pots in the kitchen. Also, I hadn't told my friends what Mom said about maybe not performing. But I hoped we could find a variable for our science project today. Then I'd still be able to play at the banquet.

"Anything happening?" I asked everybody.

They all shook their heads.

Kevin rubbed the goo off his hands onto a paper towel. "I think the dirt one is cool."

I rolled my eyes. "But nothing changed," I pointed out. "It just made the goo dirty."

Kevin shrugged. "Still."

"What if you do something with the goo?" asked Jasmine. She rubbed her hands on a paper towel, too. "You know, to see what it does? Maybe that could be your variable."

"Like what?" I asked.

Becca grinned. "Maybe we should throw it."

"Throw it?!" I gaped at her.

"Yeah, cool!" said Kevin.

Becca and Kevin picked up handfuls of their goo.

"Wait, stop—" I said. But I was too late.

Two big clumps of goo went *splat!* right on the sidewalk.

"Look what you did!" I shouted at them.

Becca's shoulders slumped. "Sorry," she said. "I was just trying to help."

"Well, you're not. You're just making a mess!" I felt tears in my eyes. "This project is important!" I ran toward my house. I didn't want to cry in front of everybody.

"Maggie, wait! Are we still on for practice Monday?" Becca called.

But I pretended I hadn't heard her. I kept running till I was inside.

We were never going to find a variable now!

DRUM SOLO

Dad calls our basement a minefield. The toys always trip him. My drum set is in the far corner, so I have to cross the minefield to get there.

That Sunday afternoon, I stepped over Megan's dolls, hopped over her trains, and navigated around Morgan's blocks.

I plopped down at the drum set and breathed out a sigh of relief.

There was less than a week left till the banquet. I hadn't heard from my friends since the goo disaster yesterday. I was sure they all sounded great on "Sound of Stardust," but I sure didn't.

Right now though, I just needed to play.

A bowl of goo sat on the table across the room. I felt like it was laughing at me.

Ugh, I thought. I just needed to forget that science project for a while!

The picture of my dad on the wall stared down at me. In the photo, he was sitting behind his old drum set. He always told me the same thing about the drums: focus on one thing at a time.

I started a beat on the kick drum. No problem there.

Then I added in the high hat every other beat. Easy.

And then quick taps on the ride cymbal.

I grinned. I sped up, faster and faster. It was getting closer to being right.

I pretended Becca was playing her guitar solo. I hit accents for it on the high hat.

Then it was my turn.

I hit the toms and spun the sticks. I hit the crash for a big finish.

"Yes!" I yelled. I had no audience except Megan's dolls. But I'd gotten the drum part to "Sound of Stardust" right for the first time! I smiled up at the picture of my dad.

I couldn't wait to show him the band!

THE GOO
GOES AWOL

"Your friends are downstairs," Mom said the next day after school. "Are you going to practice with them?"

I set my backpack down and slapped my forehead. Right. It was Monday. Practice at my house. I took a deep breath. "Yeah," I told her.

I shuffled to the top of the stairs and peeked down.

"I'm going to wear my new purple sequin dress!" I heard Scarlet say. "Aunt Billie and Kyle got it for me."

"I have a sparkly pink dress," said Jasmine. "We should all wear sparkly dresses!"

Becca frowned. "I don't have a sparkly dress."

Scarlet shrugged.

"Oh well," she said.

"Just a fancy dress then."

She and Scarlet bounced up and down in excitement.

I thought of the two dresses in my closet. Neither one sparkled. Neither one was fancy. Mom already thought I shouldn't play at the banquet. There was no way she'd buy me a new dress for it.

I took a breath and went downstairs.

My friends got quiet when they saw me.

"I'm sorry I yelled at you," I told Becca. My lower lip quivered. Maybe I'd just run back upstairs. I could cry in my room and no one would hear me.

"It's okay," she said. "I'm sorry we threw the goo without asking."

"What's the matter, Maggie?" asked Scarlet.

A single tear slid down my cheek. It was time to tell them. "My mom won't let me play at the banquet."

"What?!" they all said.

I sniffed. "Unless my science project is done. And we still don't have a variable!"

"This is not good," Scarlet said. "We can't play that song without you."

Jasmine put a hand on my shoulder. "Maybe we can try to help you again."

"Yeah," Scarlet and Becca said together.

"Thanks, guys," I said. "But I'm not sure what you can do."

"I'm sure we'll think of something," said Jasmine. "Let's practice first. Then at least we'll be ready for the banquet." She sat down behind her keyboard.

I sniffed and nodded. But then something made me frown.

"Hey, have you guys seen my goo?" I spun around, searching the room. "It's gone AWOL!"

"What's that mean?" said Scarlet.

I lifted the lid on the toy chest and peered inside. No goo there. "Absent without leave. It means missing."

We all poked around the basement. It wasn't on the table. It wasn't on the floor. It wasn't on the toy shelves.

Just then, Kevin's sneakers stomped down the stairs.

"Hey, Maggie," he said. "Do you want to work on the project?" He saw my friends and his face got red. "Oh, sorry."

"It's okay," I said. "We were just practicing for the banquet."

His eyes lit up. "Cool! Can I watch?"

"We've never had anyone watch our rehearsal before," Jasmine whispered.

I took a deep breath. "He's a musician, too. Can he stay?"

Becca shrugged. "Fine by me."

"All right," sighed Scarlet.

"I guess," said Jasmine.

"Great!" said Kevin. He sat down cross-legged on the carpet.

I kept craning my neck around to look for the goo as I set up behind the drum set. I hoped my mom hadn't thrown it out.

Scarlet turned on the mic. I flicked on the sound system.

Jasmine played the opening notes.

My sticks were ready. I checked the speaker behind me. And then my mouth opened in horror.

My sisters had set up a play kitchen. They had turned the speaker over, with its cone portion pointing upward.

And sitting in the middle of the speaker cone was our goo!

DANCING GOO

Becca started her guitar part. I wasn't sure what to do.

Speakers are expensive. Mom and I have strict rules about using the sound system.

The goo being inside the speaker cone was definitely against the rules!

I didn't have time to think. When the band starts a song, I have to come in on cue. So, I started the kick drum.

And then, a miracle happened.

The goo began to dance!

It formed little spikes. Then the spikes changed shape. They joined together and bounced up and down.

My mouth dropped open.

Scarlet sang, "It's midnight and the sky is clear . . . I can't go back to bed . . . the sky is keeping me awake . . . the sound of stardust in my head. . . ."

"What are you guys doing?" yelled Becca. She stopped playing. But the goo kept right on dancing.

Jasmine quit playing to get a better look.

The goo didn't stop dancing.

I dropped my sticks and took my foot off the kick pedal. The goo melted into a puddle again.

"It's only when *you* play," Kevin said, pointing at me. "Keep playing!"

I fumbled for my sticks and hit the bass drum.

The goo began to dance again.

The other Major Eights gathered around to get a closer look.

"Wow!" they yelled.

"But why does it only like me?" I asked.

"It's the drums," shouted Kevin. "Watch." He motioned for me to scoot over. I gave him my sticks. He kept time on the kick drum, then added in the snare and the toms.

Kevin was pretty good.

He played louder, and the goo went crazy. It formed a lump. The lump jumped around in time with the drums. He laughed. "We can use sound as our variable!"

"Ooh! I have an amazing idea!" I squealed. "But we're going to need help," I said to my friends.

"We're in!" they shouted.

BEHIND THE CURTAIN

"Is it all ready?" I asked Becca.

She saluted me. "I brought the three speakers up front. Just like you said."

Scarlet spun in a circle. Her purple dress sparkled. "Like it?"

"Oh, Scarlet, it's so pretty!" said Jasmine. She twirled in her pink dress.

Becca smoothed out the black satin on her outfit. "I hate dresses! You guys are lucky I have one."

I tugged at my white sundress. It wasn't special, but I was just glad Mom had let me play. She'd even hired a babysitter, so both she and Nana could come. But Nana had said she had an errand to run first.

Kevin joined us. He wore jeans, a collared shirt, and a bow tie. "Are we ready?" he asked.

We nodded.

I peeked out from behind the curtain. Round tables filled the gym floor. Paper stars hung from the ceiling. The audience wore suits and fancy dresses. Becca's mom had set out flowers on the tables. Waiters laid out plates of food. My mom chatted with another parent at her table. Though Nana still wasn't with her.

Mr. Caldera saw me from his seat and waved.

I waved back, then closed the curtain, clutching the speech he had helped me write.

Nana rushed backstage.

"Nana! What are you doing here?" I asked. "It's almost time for the show to start!"

The tap dancers clacked onto the stage. The emcee quieted the crowd. She was giving a speech to thank everyone for coming. Then the clacks began.

Nana thrust a bag at me. "I took off the tags," she said. "Quick! Go change."

"Change . . . ?"
But Nana scooted me off.

In the bathroom, I opened the bag. My eyes got as big as speaker cones.

While I changed, the tap dancers stopped. The audience clapped. The magician was up next, and we were after him.

When I came out, my friends' mouths popped open.

"Nice dress!" said Scarlet.

I felt the smooth, navy blue fabric. Silver sequins were sewn all over it. I grinned. "Just like the stars, Nana!"

"Just like you, sweetie." Nana smiled. "It looks lovely with your red hair. Now go get ready. I've got to join your mother."

"Thank you so much, Nana!"

I hugged her and she left through a back door.

"Is the goo all set up?" I asked Kevin.

"Yep," he said. "I covered the speaker cones with plastic this time. I never want to scrape dried goo out of a speaker again."

I giggled. "Yeah. Good thinking."

Applause drifted backstage. The magician was finished with his act.

"Places!" I called to my friends.

Becca strapped on her guitar. Jasmine hurried to the keyboard. Scarlet stepped back from the mic, letting Kevin and me stand there first.

The emcee said, "And now . . . the Major Eights!"

The curtain whooshed back.

There were a lot of people in the audience. Usually, I'm at the back behind my drum set so I don't feel like I have a hundred eyes all on me. But this time, I was standing front and center, about to speak into the mic to the entire audience.

Then I spotted my mom. She was watching, but she didn't have her phone out.

She had to take a video! That was the whole point!

I thought fast, but I had no way to remind her.

All my hard work was about to be for nothing!

THE BEST SURPRISE

Kevin covered the mic with one of his hands before either of us spoke into it. "What's up?" he whispered to me.

"My mom said she'd take a video. I just saw her. She's not doing it."

"Don't worry," he said. "My mom can send hers to your mom."

I swallowed. "Thanks."

It still didn't make sense. Mom knew how important this was.

"I . . . um . . . hi," I said into the mic. "I'm Maggie. And this is Kevin. We're both drummers."

"We decided to do our science project on music," Kevin added, stepping forward.

I smiled. "And we'd like to share it with all of you."

Mr. Caldera winked from the audience.

"There are three speakers." Kevin pointed. "Each has a mixture of cornstarch and water in it. Our goo likes to dance. But not to everything."

"We wanted to know what kind of sounds made it dance the most," I said. "So, we made sound our variable. The first speaker is for high sounds, like Scarlet's voice. The second is for ones in the middle, like the guitar and keyboard. And the third is for low sounds. It's connected to the mic at the drum set."

"Watch the goo dance along as the Major Eights play 'Sound of Science,'" Kevin said. He hurried backstage to watch.

I took my place behind the drums. Jasmine began her keyboard intro. Becca came in on guitar.

I started the kick drum.

The goo in the third speaker began to bounce. People in the audience stood up for a better view. Several came closer to watch.

Scarlet sang, "It's midnight and the sky is clear . . . I can't go back to bed . . . a question's keeping me awake . . . the sound of science in my head. . . . "

The audience laughed. They knew the Silver Sporks song, and they liked our changes to it.

I grinned at Scarlet, Jasmine, and Becca. They grinned back.

The audience crowded around the stage. It felt like a real concert. When we hit my solo, the goo in the third speaker went crazy! It wiggled around. It jiggled. It almost looked like someone dancing!

When we finished, the crowd erupted into loud cheering.

The emcee took over. "The Major Eights, everyone!"

The audience whistled. Everyone was still on their feet.

My friends and I clasped hands. I waved Kevin back onstage and he took a bow with us.

"We did it, Maggie!" He gave me a high five.

"You were right," I admitted. "Music does have science in it. I'm sorry I didn't believe you."

"No worries." He smiled at me. I felt glad we'd become friends.

Mr. Caldera met me backstage. "Well," he whispered, "I know the science fair isn't until Monday, but it's safe to say that you two earned an A+ on this project. Well done!"

I bounced up and down, grinning.

"Yes!" yelled Kevin.

Jasmine, Becca, and Scarlet crowded in. They patted the both of us on the back.

Then Mom and Nana came over.

"Mom!" I said. "Why didn't you take a video for Dad?"

Mom smiled. "I didn't need to," she said, pointing.

A man in uniform stepped out from the crowd.

"Dad?!" I gasped.

"Hey, Mag-o!" Dad picked me up and swung me around.

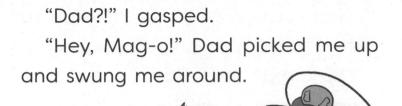

"Surprise! I'm on leave early."

"I didn't want to spoil the surprise," said Mom.

"Did you see us perform?" I asked him.

"Sure did," said Dad. "You did an amazing job, kiddo!" He handed me a bouquet of flowers.

"Thank you, Dad. I missed you so much!"

"I missed you, too," he said. I turned to my friends.

"Thanks, guys. I couldn't have done this without you."

"I told you we could help," Jasmine said.

Kevin shifted his feet nearby. We pulled him into a group hug.

"So," said Dad, "Will we hear more from the Major Eights?"

I grinned at my friends and they grinned back.

"Yeah," I said. "We're just getting started!"

MAKE YOUR OWN GOO!

Would you like to make goo, too? It's easy! Just be sure to get a grown-up to help.

YOU WILL NEED:
- a measuring cup
- a medium mixing bowl
- a spoon
- 2 cups cornstarch
- 1 cup water

HOW TO MAKE IT:
1. Measure out the cornstarch and water and add them to the mixing bowl.
2. Mix with the spoon—but you won't get too far before you'll want to mix with your hands!

TRY THIS:

- Shape your goo into a ball. What happens when you drop it?
- Pound the goo with your fist. Then slowly stick one of your fingers into it.

Which of these methods do you find easier to do?

To Make Goo Dance on a Speaker:
(ONLY DO THIS WITH A GROWN-UP'S HELP!)
Note: A subwoofer, a special speaker made for very low sounds, works best for this.

1. Turn the speaker on its back, with the speaker cone facing up.
2. ALWAYS cover the speaker cone and the surface around the cone with plastic cling wrap! You'll ruin the speaker if you don't.
3. Mix your goo in a separate bowl, then pour it into the wrapped speaker cone.
4. Ask a grown-up to loosen the goo from the sides of the wrapped speaker cone with a spoon. Be gentle!
5. Turn on music with a good bass line.
6. Now watch your goo dance to the music!

Read on for a sneak peek from the fourth book in THE MAJOR EiGHTS series, *Starstruck.*

THE MAJOR EIGHTS

STARSTRUCK

BOOK
4

THE WALL OF FAME

As soon as Mom parked the car in front of our house, I undid my seat belt and threw open the door. I was running late for band practice with the Major Eights.

"Becca," Mom called. "Don't forget to take your trash."

"But, Mom," I said, "I'm late!"

"Your friends can wait two minutes."

My big brothers, Lucas and Manny, hopped out of the car.

"Whoops," said Manny. "I can't forget this!" He grabbed a gold basketball trophy from the backseat.

Lucas whooped. "Uh-huh. Two more trophies for the Wall!"

I frowned at my brothers. "Hey, my team was pretty close!" But Lucas and Manny were already almost inside the house and didn't hear me.

I wadded up my hot dog wrapper in a fist and ran after them.

From the front door, I heard Jasmine playing chords in my family's garage. Scarlet sang scales. Maggie played a solo on the drum set. I quickly disposed of my trash and raced to the garage.

My family doesn't park our cars in our garage. A shag rug covers the floor. An old sofa sits against the far wall. My oldest brother, Tony, has an old guitar that sits in one corner. Along another whole wall runs my family's Wall of Fame. It has tons of awards and trophies. All of them belong to my three big brothers.

"I'm here!" I announced to my friends. "What did I miss?"

"Hey, Becca!" said Maggie. "You're just in time!"

"Is basketball season over now?" asked Scarlet.

"How was your last game?" asked Jasmine.

"Yeah, it was our last game," I said. "It went great! We didn't win, though."

"Maybe next year," said Jasmine.

I nodded. I took my place with the band, facing the Wall of Fame. Lucas and Manny had already added their new trophies to it. The only thing I had up there was a poster. It wasn't signed, like my brothers' posters on the Wall. But it was a picture of Lucy "the Leaper" Landon. Lucy was the best point guard in the world. She played on the basketball team at Center State University. I got to see her play a few months ago.

"Are you guys ready to practice?" Jasmine asked. "I think 'Take My Shot' is really sounding good."

"Yeah!" said Scarlet.

"Ready!" said Maggie.

"Sure," I said, still gazing over at the poster.

My friends waited.

"Oh, right." I grabbed a guitar pick. "I start this one."

I played the first chords.

Scarlet sang, "It's time . . . to take my shot. . . ."

As I strummed, I continued to stare at the poster.

I didn't have any trophies on the Wall—yet. But with basketball season over, I wouldn't be adding any to the Wall soon. But a signed poster would be even better than a trophy.

If only I could find a way to meet Lucy.